# The Windy Day

# The Wet Day

# The Warm Day

For little Alice McKeown

P. G.


For everyone who helped

along the way

A. C.

# The Windy Day

'What a windy day!' said Miss Chutney
as she hung out her washing.
Whoops! Off flew one sock, then two!

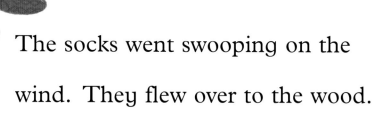

The socks went swooping on the wind. They flew over to the wood. One landed on Squirrel. Flap!

One landed on Mouse. Flop!

8

'Just what I need!' said Squirrel.

'A hat.'

'A sleeping bag to keep me warm!'

said Mouse.

The wind blew and blew, and . . .

Off flew more of Miss Chutney's

washing.

It all went into the wood.

It got dark. The wind blew under Miss Chutney's door. Wheeew!

Miss Chutney was cold without her blanket. Shiver shiver.

But the animals
and birds were warm
under and in and on the
big tree in the wood.

13

WHEEEW! The wind blew harder.

The big tree began to creak.

Creak creak CRASH SMASH!

Mouse and Squirrel and Owl and
Fox went up the hill.

Knock knock!

Soon nobody was cold
any more.

Snore!

# The Wet Day

Split-splat!

It was a wet day outside and inside

Miss Chutney's house.

'Oh no, the roof has got a hole in it!'
said Miss Chutney.

Crash!

Some of the roof fell on to the floor.

Split-splat-splot!

'I haven't got enough money
to pay a builder to mend it!' said
Miss Chutney. 'Now I have nowhere
to live!'

'Don't worry,' said Fox. 'We will all help to get the money to pay for a new roof. You helped us, and we will help you.'

'We can sell things,' said Owl.

Fox and Squirrel took all

Miss Chutney's furniture outside.

Mouse made a sign.

Nobody wanted to buy anything.

'It is all too tatty,' said

Miss Chutney.

'Don't worry,' said Squirrel.

'We will make it all nicer.'

Mouse and Squirrel and Owl and

Fox set to work.

Soon everybody wanted to buy things. Miss Chutney had enough money to pay the builder.

There was even enough money left over to pay for buns for tea.

Hooray!

It's even better than it was before!

# The Warm Day

Miss Chutney and Mouse and Owl and Fox and Squirrel had a nice house to live in.

But it was an empty house.

What can we sit on?

'We must make new furniture,' said

Miss Chutney. 'I have an idea.

Follow me!'

Miss Chutney took some tools.

Off they went to the wood.

'We will make your old home into things for our new home,' Miss Chutney told the animals.

They all set to work again.

Fox made bowls and cups.

Miss Chutney cut logs to make a

table and stools.

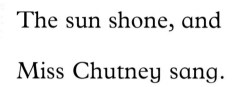

The sun shone, and

Miss Chutney sang.

Saw,
Saw,
Let's make
some
more!

Squirrel and Mouse wove hammocks

for beds.

Owl made a broom to sweep
the house clean.

Miss Chutney put soil into a pot.

Then she put in something else.

'It's a seed. It needs soil and water and sunshine, and then it will grow into a new tree,' said Miss Chutney. 'When it is big enough, we will plant it in the wood where your old tree was.'

47

That made Mouse and Fox and Owl and Squirrel and all the birds and animals very happy.

And Miss Chutney was happy too.